Lidija Šimkutė*White Shadows / 白い影

Lidija Šimkutė : Weiße Schatten / White Shadows
edition selene, Wien 2000

Erstausgabe
Layout: Ribert Sphinxfield

© Lidija Šimkutė
© 2000 für die Übersetzung: edition selene, Wien, Austria
© Zeichnungen von / artwork by Slava Karmalita

Lidija Šimkutė

Weiße Schatten
White Shadows

白い影

Aus dem Englischen von
Christian Loidl

日本語訳
薬師川虹一

c h i k u r i n k a n

Touching Silence.

Lidija Šimkutė's poetry is elemental. Its themes – wo /man, faced with impermanence, solitude, love, landscape, language versus silence – are neither new nor dated. The value of such poetry today depends on the poet's ability to replace the known with discovery, arbitrariness with intensity. Šimkutė's poems merge passion with abstraction, or concreteness with reduction. Her language does not exhaust itself in mere representation nor does it dissolve into the formless. Šimkutė's poetry moves on the border of disappearance like a Buto dancer above an abyss: *MY SECRET // A fragile longing / In hands / White / Crumbling / Paper.*

The poems strike faster than thought. Like totems, masks, and like the cyclical, non-linear vocal music of Lithuania, they evoke a world which is ancient, young and utterly vivid. They do without wordplay, idiosyncrasy, and extravaganza. They are essences and formulas.

Šimkutė's language is a subtle instrument of emotional nuance. It lacks the relativism of postmodern thought, and the questioning of language as conditioned by time and convention. Language becomes a theme only in an existential context: that is, when questioned as to whether it is an adequate means for conveying experience or just another kind of muteness.

At first glance, Šimkutė's poems evoke silence. Silence becomes audible when the poet gets on stage. It is a meditative quality, which communicates before speech

沈黙に触れる

　リジア・シュムクーテの詩は根源的である。その主題―不確定、孤独、愛、風景、言葉対沈黙という問題に向き合うときの人間―は新しいものでもなく古びたものでもない。こういう問題を扱う詩の価値は見慣れたものを異様なものに、恣意を真意に置き換えうる力を詩人が持っているかどうかにかかっている。

　シュムクーテの詩は感動と抽象を、不動と流動を、溶融する。彼女の言葉は単なる言い換えに終始するものではなく、とりとめのないものになって消えていくものでもない。シュムクーテの詩は幽玄の極で流動する。それはまるで奈落の淵で舞う舞妓に似ている。

　私の秘密は // 儚い願い / 掌中の / 崩れる / 白い / 紙

　彼女の詩は思考より早く心に届く。トーテムや偶像、または、ひたすら伸びる線ではなく回転しながら歌われるリトアニアの歌曲のように、古代から続き今も若々しく生き生きとしている世界を呼び起こすのだ。それは言葉遊びではなく、彼女の特異体質でもなく、狂想劇でもない。彼女の詩は本質を突き、枠組みの中にある。

　シュムクーテの言葉は微妙な楽器のように心に響く陰影を持っている。それはポストモダニズムの持つ相対主義を拒否する。それは、言葉が時代と因習とによって定まるという疑念を拒否する。言葉は実存の脈絡においてのみ主体となりうる、即ち、言葉が経験を伝えるための適切な手段であるかそれともまったく異なる沈黙であるべきかが問われるときにおいてのみ言葉は主題となりうるのである。

　一見すれば、シュムクーテの詩は沈黙を呼び起こす。しかしその沈黙は詩人が登場するとき響き始める。その本質は想念である。それは言葉が概念となる前に伝わるのだ。それは判ると思う時でさえ

becomes concept. And it remains, even when one thinks one understands. How does this quality come about? Perhaps it is a piece of heritage from Lithuania's wise-women, or from a pre-sanskrit world-view, which pervades Lithuania to this day.

Although Šimkutė has been living in Australia since her childhood, her first books of poetry were written in Lithuanian. She has cherished Lithuanian culture as almost a mythical reference. This may be due to her upbringing, in which that culture and language were nurtured, while the land and its people were occupied and persecuted to the point of genocide by the Soviet system.

Her father, originally a farmer, was well read, a great story-teller and occasional writer, while the mother kept up many Lithuanian traditions in the household, such as weaving and baking bread.

When Šimkutė decided to write in her mother tongue, she extended her language by correspondence in Lithuanian literature, history and folklore through the Lithuanian Language Institute in Chicago, where the largest émigré population lived. With political changes, the opportunity arose to further her studies in Lithuania and to establish contact with poets and artists as well as with her relatives. The theme of isolation, loss and longing pervades much of her earlier work. It is usually expressed as a dialectical tension, which sometimes results in an identification of opposites. Thus loss may, on another level, become gain:

I WAS USED TO MY WALLS / You wrecked them and enclosed me / Within Yourself.

想念のままなのだ。こういう性質はどうして生まれてくるのだろう
か？　おそらくそれはリトアニアの賢女たちから伝わる一つの遺産
かそれともサンスクリット時代以前から今日もなおリトアニアに伝
わる世界観からの遺産ではなかろうか。

　シュムクーテは彼女の少女時代からオーストラリアで暮らしてい
るが、彼女の最初の詩集はリトアニア語で書かれている。彼女はリ
トアニアの伝統文化を不思議な参考書として大切に抱えてきた。こ
れはおそらく彼女の育ちのせいだろう。その中でそういう文化と言
葉が育まれ、その一方でこの国と国民はソビエトの体制に占領され、
ほとんど壊滅に近いほど迫害されていたのだ。

　彼女の父親は教育があり、お話が上手で、時々物語を書いたりし
ていた。一方母親は織物をしたり、パンを焼くなど様々なリトアニ
アの伝統的な作業を家庭の中で守り続けていた。

　シュムクーテが母国語で詩を書こうと決心したころ、シカゴにあ
るリトアニア文化学院で改めてリトアニアの文学、歴史、民話など
に触れ、彼女の言葉の世界は一層広がっていった。シカゴには非常
に多くの国からの移民たちが暮らしていたことも大きな影響を与え
た。

　政治状況の変化につれリトアニア国について学ぶ機会が多くなり、
親類縁者たちとのつながりとともに詩人たちやその他芸術家たちと
の付き合いも増えてきた。それとともに彼女の初期の作品の多くに
孤立や喪失、憧れといったテーマが増えていった。それらは大体弁
証法的な緊張状態として現れ、時として対立するものの同一化と
なって表現される。こうして喪失は別の次元で獲得となって表れる。

　私は自分の壁に慣れていた / 貴方はその壁を破り私を閉じ込めた
/ 貴方自身の中に

What is meant by You remains open. The poem in its elementary structure can express several meanings. The You can apply to a human being, a continent, a meta-physical being. Here, as in many other instances, Šimkutė's poetry possesses a form of polyvalence that is found in mystical language. The physical cannot be clearly segregated from the metaphysical; one may signify the other. Equally open are the boundaries between the individual and nature:

IN MY SECRET PLACES / *Stir the waves of the sea* // *In the waves of the sea* / *Stirs the beginning.*

Such correspondence between physical, psychological and cosmic elements are characteristic of cultures in which the sacred and the natural, the vital and the spiritual are close to each other or even identical. The correspondence between *my secret places*, *the waves of the sea* and *the beginning* are archetypal and cannot be reduced to one conceptual meaning. Their flow is reflected in the structure of the poem, which resembles the movement between one wave and another wave, with silence or an empty moment in between.

It is, generally, a delicate border that separates an archetype from a cliché. In Šimkutė's work however, even much-used images and words (such as *sea* or *wave* or *beginning*) succeed in making the known into a vehicle of the unknown. Thus the imagination truly touches upon a beginning, an openness, something that remains unhampered by the usual:

No longer the sea flows, but I flow / *No longer the sun warms, but I warm* // *And no wave can erase* / *My imprint in the sand.*

ここで「貴方」が何を意味するかは漠然としている。この詩の基本的な構造からして、この詩はいくつかの意味を表現しうるといえる。この「貴方」という言葉は「一人の人」「一つの大陸」「何か形而上的存在」にも当てはめうるだろう。他にも多々みられるのだが、シュムクーテの詩は様々に解釈しうる顔を持っているのであり、それは神秘的な言葉によくみられるものなのだ。そこでは具象と非具象とを分けることができず、互いに相手を表現しあっているのである。同様に個体と人自然との境界も存在しない。

　私の秘め処で / 波がしらがうごめき // 波がしらの中で / 太初があふれる

　肉体的、心理的、宇宙的諸要素の相関関係の中で文化の本質が形成され、そこでは聖なるものと自然なもの、生と聖、肉と霊は互いに密となり、ついには同一とさえなる。呼応しあう私の秘所、海のうねり、太初は原型的存在であり一つの概念的指示物に矮小化され得ないものなのだ。この三者の繋がりはこの詩の構造となり、その動きは一つのうねりと次のうねりとの間に静寂あるいは空白を伴っているのに似ている。

　概して言えば、原型と慣習とを分ける線は微妙なものであろう。しかしながらシュムクーテの場合、使い古されたイメージや単語でさえ（例えば、*海、波、太初、*といった言葉でさえ）既知のものを未知のものに繋ぐ道具として成功している。こうして彼女のイマジネーションは太初とか無辺とか、何か日常的なものによって封じ込められていないものに繋っているのである。

　もはや海は溢れず溢れるのは私 / もはや太陽は温めず温めるのは私 // 砂に刻んだ足跡を / 波も消すことはできない

It may be safely assumed that, in addition to Šimkutė's Lithuanian roots, it was the expansiveness of the Australian continent that has imprinted itself profoundly onto her work, instilling luminosity and space.

Šimkutė's particular quality is in opening language into vastness, even at moments when the emotions expressed are of darkness and barrenness:

I absorb light / Like a fruitless field.

Just as poetic language gains its force by evading the usual and the merely discursive, so persons in Šimkutė's work sometimes attain a paradoxical presence in their absence or in their non-being. Elsewhere becomes here, things become a language of love:

I touch grass / Leaves of trees / A stone // But yearn / For your touch.

Reading Šimkutė's verse, one may be reminded of Japan and its poetry, where one luminous image surrounded by silence can say so much more than a million words.

Cut hair / Touched by your lips / blew on stone.

Christian Loidl

シュムクーテの持つリトアニア的風土に加えて、オーストラリア大陸の風土が持つ広大さを考慮することは当然であろう。それは彼女の詩的世界に深く沁み込み明るさと広がりを与えている。
シュムクーテの特性は言葉に無限の広がりを与えていることにある。たとえそこに表現されている情感が暗く不毛なものであるときでさえそうなのだ。

　　私は光を吸い込む / まるで涸れた畑

　詩の言葉がありきたりの言葉や、単に述べるだけの言葉であることを避けることによって力を得ているように、彼女の詩に登場する人物は時に姿を消し、或いは非在の存在になることによって逆説的な存在となりうるのである。何処は此処となり、物象は睦語となる：

　　私が触れるのは草 / 木の葉 / 石ころ // だけど欲しいのは / あなたの肌ざわり

　シュムクーテの詩を読んでいると読者は日本を想いその詩を想いおこすだろう。そこでは沈黙に閉ざされることによって一つのイメージが輝き、百万の言葉よりはるかに多くのことが語られるのである。

　　髪を切り / あなたの唇に触れ / 石に吹きつける

　　クリスチャン・ロイデル

Christian Loidl
オーストリアの詩人（1957−2001）。イカロスのような生涯だったと言われている。
彼の言葉に、「凝視するに値するものは、凝視し得ないものだ」というのがある。

A white flower grows in the quietness
let your tongue become that flower

Jelaluddin Rumi

We count on blood resembling blood
in our thirst for silence

Edmond Jabès

白い花が一輪静かに開く
貴方の言葉をその白い花にせよ

ジャラールディーン・ルーミー

私たちは似た者同士の血に頼り
沈黙を渇望する

エドモン・ジャベス

Jelaluddin Rumi
13世紀のペルシャの神秘的詩人（1207-1273）。

Edmond Jabès
エジプトの詩人(1912-1991)。1912年イタリア系ユダヤ人としてカイロに生まれる。
1757年エジプトを去り、フランスに住む。

THE SECOND LONGING
二度目の願い

IN MY SECRET PLACES
Stir the waves of the sea

In the waves of the sea
Flows the beginning

私の秘め処で
波がしらがうごめき

波がしらの中で
太初があふれる

THE STRETCH OF THE SEA

Strange and familiar faces
Search for lost paths in water

Unseen doors slam
Windows of thought melt

Clouds break up
The sun's rays turn into snowflakes

張り詰める海

見たこともない親しげな顔が
水に消えた小道を探している

見えないドアがピシャリと閉まり
想いの窓は溶けていく

雲は千切れ
陽光は雪片々

YOU COME
Hesitate
Then pass

That is
My eternity

貴方は来る
ためらい
そして去る

それが私の
永遠

I WANT NOT WORDS
But eyes and flesh to speak
So that in coming together

There'll be no room for promises

I WAS USED TO MY WALLS
You wrecked them and enclosed me
within yourself

言葉なんかいらない
語ってくれる瞳と身体
だからさあ行きましょう

約束の余地などないの

私は自分の壁に慣れていた
貴方はその壁を破り私を閉じ込めた
貴方自身の中に

NIGHT AND SEA

Wind and sky
Sun and clouds
   have rejected me

Earth alone pulls
   my hand to herself

夜も海も

風も空も
陽も雲も
　私を拒んできた

大地だけが私の手を
　その身に引きよせてくれる

IN THE HOUSE
Unfamiliar light and smells

Near a long oak table
A fallen chair prayed

The sound of
Satie: Gymnopédies

The dog barked
The storm came
Pictures darkened

A silhouette passed
Half lit by cold stars

家の内で
不気味な光と臭い

長い樫のテーブルの傍
倒れた椅子が祈っている

サティの音色
ジムノペディ

犬が吠え
嵐が襲い
絵は黒ずみ

影が一つよぎり
星は冷たく仄か

サティ　Erik Alfred Leslie Satie
フランスの作曲家（1866－1925）。ジムノペディ（Gymnopédies）は彼のピアノ小曲。

HUNGER PROWLS THE GRASS

The sky is pale

Clouds bony and lean

Winter eats the sun

        from my palm

The wind hides

Unbreathing

In the valley

草原を徘徊する飢餓
空は青ざめ
雲は骨ばり痩せ
冬が私の掌から
　　　　太陽を食べる

風は息を
ひそめて
谷間に潜む

IN THE BACKDROP OF BLUE

Shadows stretch
Across trodden grass

Time steals the flow
          of my unlived day

Longing flows
          into distance

背景の青い幕の中で

踏みつぶされた草原を越え
いくつもの影が伸びる

時が盗むのは溢れ出る
　　　　　　私のまだ見ぬ日

憧れが遥か彼方に
　　　　　流れ去る

I WANTED
TO PLUCK YOU A SUNBEAM

But the clouds came

I wanted
To gather raindrops
And send them to you

But they dried up in my hands

私はあなたに
陽光を摘んであげたかった

でも雲が湧いてきた

雨粒を集めて
それをあなたに
送りたかった

でもそれは私の掌のなかで干あがってしまった

THE SUN IS IMPOTENT
in the icy sky

It throws thorns
But my body is stone

I stretch my hands
Towards the face that surrounds me
It has cadaver skin
and sightless eyes

I shut myself within four walls
Ceilings snow endlessly

Windows slam
Doors disappear at dusk

I suffocate

なすすべもない太陽が
　　　凍った空にいる

太陽が刺を投げるが
私の身体は石

私を取り巻く
顔に向かい両手を広げて差し出す
その肌は屍色
　　　　　目に光はない

私は四方の壁の中に閉じこもり
雪は果てしなく空を覆う

窓は閉ざされ
扉は薄暮の中に消え

私は息を止める

WALLS NOT WINDOWS
         bear secrets

Witnesses of thought
Which our lips have forgotten

Irrevocable words
Have left permanent scars

These dark keys
In the doors of night

窓ではなく壁が
　　　秘密を抱える

唇が忘れてしまった想いの
目撃者たち

取り戻せぬ言葉たちは
消えることなき傷跡を残す

夜の扉の
暗い鍵たち

I WANT TO
Open clenched fists
And look into the palm

So that when we part
I will know
The maps of grace

私は握りこぶしを開いて
手の内を
覗いてみたい

別れる時
癒しの地図を
見たいから

WHEN WE OVERCOME
ALL OBSTACLES

And there is nothing
        separating us

For sweat like an iron cable
Unites our bodies

Suddenly
There arises

The Uncrossable Wall of China
And with it comes

The Second Longing

すべての障害を
　　　乗り越えれば

私たちを引き離すものは
一つもない

なぜなら汗が鉄の鎖のように
二人の体を繋いでいるから

いきなり
せりあがるのは

越すに越せない万里の長城
それとともに沸き起こる

二度目の願い

YOU DEPART

But do not let go

Leave the keys
Yet take the door

貴方は出て行く

けど出させない

鍵は残しているけど
しっかりドアを握っている

LET US PART
in silence

Invite no words as witnesses

Let outstretched arms
Remain in our glances

Perhaps
If we meet

In the depth of our eyes
We may no longer find
What has driven us apart

別れましょ
　　黙って

言葉を証人にしないで

広げた両腕を
目の奥に残しましょ

たぶん
私たちが

目の奥で出会っても
私たちを引き裂いたものを
見つけることはないでしょう

WITH SILENCE
I encase your words
In silence
I receive your body

Together we become
Silence

IF CLOUDS SHOULD
Touch me

I would disappear

沈黙と一緒に
あなたの言葉を胸に収め
黙って
貴方の身体を受け入れる

私たちは一緒に
沈黙となる

もし雲がひょっとして
私に触れるなら

私は消えてしまうよ

HANDS BECOME WIND

手は風になる

THE SUN PAINTS A SASH
on the floor

Colours are reborn

Ceilings wake
Drawers yawn from cupboards

The morning chooses its garments
For the day

太陽が床の上に
　　　　斜めにかかる綬章を描く

彩色がよみがえる

天井が目覚め
食器棚から引き出しが欠伸をする

朝が昼間の衣装を
選んでいる

OUTSIDE

I break a Japonica branch
Scoop up the sun

Afraid of losing
                    the day

WE LED SHADOWS
To the gate

Our thoughts
Faded the path

庭先で

私は椿の枝を折って
太陽を掬い上げる

明るい一日を
　　　　　　失わないように

私たちの影を入り口へ
連れてゆく

二人の想いが
小道に消えた

WE SHALL NOT RETURN

We shall never return
       to the unaltered past

I continue my journey
The sound of footsteps
       words
       a familiar voice

A book
Water boils
The sound of children at home

The ring of the phone
Letters
       and a chess board
       with no moves

戻ることはないだろう
変えられない過去へ
　　　　戻ることは決してないだろう

私は旅を続ける
足跡の音
　　　　　言葉
　　　　聞きなれた声

本
お湯が沸いている
伸びやかな子供たちの音

電話のベル
手紙の束
　　　　チェス盤
　　　　動かぬ駒

WITH CHILDREN'S LAUGHTER
The day began

But was stilled in the uncertainty
                of evening

I left behind
                the frayed moon

With this knife
Cut me a slice of time

I yearn for daily bread
From your hands

子供たちの笑い声で
一日が始まり

不安定な夕暮れには
　　　　　　　静まる

私は立ち去る
　　　　　後にはぼろぼろの月

このナイフで
時を一切れ切っておくれ

私はあなたの手から
今日のパンを貰いたい

BY A NARROW PATH

We climb the hill
     and reach a field
     of rocks and flowers

On drifting paths
We descend the hill
     lick salt from our lips

We listen to the wind

We tell the flowers
The secret of a drifting cloud
     and the inmost stone
     the warmth of the sun

細い小道をたどって

丘を登ると
　　　　岩と花の乱れる
　　　広場に出る

曲がりくねった小道をたどり
丘を下ってゆく
　　　　塩っぱい唇をなめながら

風の音に耳を澄ます

花たちに語り聞かせるのは
流れゆく雲の秘密
　　　　深く隠れた石には
　　　　太陽の温かさを

THE DEMENTED SEA

With white teeth
Tears at the rocks

Lightning
Has split the moon

TWILIGHT

Shattered wind

Joins the shadows

How can I put together
The sun and the moon

発狂した海が
白い歯をむいて
岩に砕ける

稲妻が
月を切り裂く

沈んだ夕陽が

風を切り刻み

夕影と合体する

どうすれば太陽と月を
合体させうるのだろう

THE DOOR SLAMS

Walls light up

The crumbs of fairy stories
        litter the table

Wind from nowhere
Blows away the last grains

ドアのしまる音

灯りに浮かび上がる壁

おとぎ話のパン屑がテーブルに
　　　散らばっている

どこからともなく吹く風が
最後のパンくずを吹き飛ばす

I LOST MY VOICE
When you leaned against it

Only an echo returned
My lips to your name

BODIES FLOAT
In word time

Where centuries
Separate word from word

私は声を失った
貴方がそれに寄り掛かったから

私の唇に帰ってくるのは
貴方の名前の木霊だけ

言葉の時代には
肉体は浮いている

幾世紀もの間
言葉と言葉は離れ離れ

SILENTLY

I meet
Your non-existence

I touch grass
Leaves of trees
A stone

But yearn
For your touch

黙って

私は向き合う
非存在の貴方に

私が触れるのは草
木の葉
石ころ

だけど欲しいのは
あなたの肌ざわり

YOUR NAME IS A DISTANT FIELD
 FLOWER

Your name is a bird in flight
Your name is white iron heat
Your name is water crystal renewal

Your name has no name

I LET YOUR NAME
Cupped tightly in my hands
Fly into the sky

貴方の名前は遠い野原の花

貴方の名前は飛んでいる鳥
貴方の名前は白熱の鉄
貴方の名前は生まれ変わった水晶

貴方の名前は名前を持たない

両手の中に
捕らえていた貴方の名前を
大空に放つ

I AM SKIN
A sensitive cloak on bone

I cover thought
Desire nothing

IN WHITE CORRIDORS
Bats play

Your black eyes
Thread silk strands

私は皮膚
骨にかぶさる敏感な肌着

私は想いを隠し
なにも願わない

白い回廊で
蝙蝠たちが遊ぶ

貴方の黒い瞳が
絹糸を編む

NIGHT IS LIGHT
For stars burn

My feelings are black
I absorb light
Like a fruitless field

THE SULLEN FRESCO
Keeps vigil in the sleeping room

Near it the spider
Weaves a Fra Angelico riddle

夜は明るい
星が燃えるから

私の心は暗い
私は光を吸い込む
まるで涸れた畑

不機嫌なフレスコ画が
寝室で見張りを続けている

そのそばで蜘蛛が
フラ・アンジェリコ風の謎を編んでいる

フラ・アンジェリコ
イタリアの画家（1395-1455）。「受胎告知」で知られる。

I CUT UP OLD PHOTOGRAPHS
Toss them into the fire

I watch them flicker and die

Embers fall to ashes
Having heard the lament

of bodies, skulls

私は古い写真を切り刻み
暖炉に投げ捨てる

それが炎を上げて死ぬのを見つめる

燃えがらが崩れて灰になる
肉と骨の嘆きが

　　　　　　聞こえた

FROM ASHES I ERECT
A STATUE

It will be completed
When hands become wind

ANCHORS

We shall never return
    to light

We shall never follow
    the path of birds

私は灰の中から一つの彫像を
立ち上げる

それは両手が風になるとき
完成されるだろう

錨

私たちは決して戻ることはないだろう
　　　　光の中へ

私たちは決して辿ることはないだろう
　　　　小鳥たちの道を

I'LL DRINK ALL TIME
Only sand will remain

Dregs of thought
Will form a monument

THE MONUMENT OF LOVE
Is a sculpture of sand

I'll drink all sand
All will remain

私はすべての時を飲み込む
残るのは砂のみ

想いの残りかすが
記念碑になるだろう

愛の記念碑は
砂の彫刻

私は砂をすべて飲み干す
すべては元のまま

MY SECRET

A fragile longing

In hands
White
Crumbling
Paper

WEAR MY MEMORY
       cast
In silence

私の秘密は

儚い願い

掌中の

崩れる

白い

紙

私の記憶をすり潰せ
　　　　　　黙って
投げ捨てろ

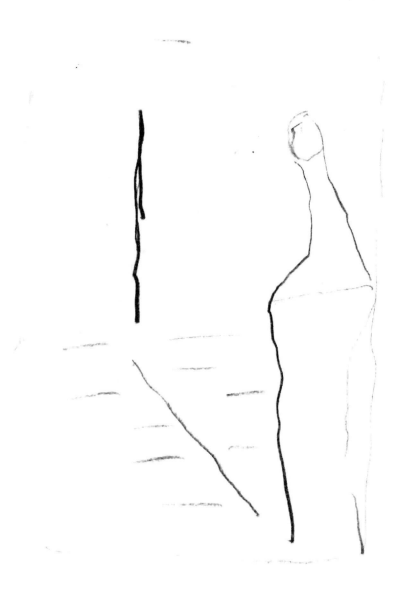

WHITE SHADOWS

白い影

BIRDS FLUTTER
Splash my blood

I'm the fruit
In the orchard

I cast away desire
Flowers and petals

鳥たちが羽ばたき
私の血を振りまく

私は果樹園の
果物

私は願望を捨てる
花も花びらも

CATCHING A GLIMPSE
Of shadows
Playing between doors

The pomegranates
Nodded their heads

SHADOWS FADED
With the tone of the guitar

Striking a window
A butterfly fell

ドアのあたりで遊んでいる
影たちの
流し目を感じて

ザクロが
頭で頷く

影は消える
ギターの調べと共に

窓にあたって
蝶が落ちた

WITHOUT A FRIEND
I'll sit
By my side
And sing a song
Heard elsewhere

In the morning
I'll swim to the sun
And dive
       beyond blue

一人の友達もなく
私は私と
並んで座り
どこかで聞いた
歌を歌う

朝
太陽に向かって私は泳ぎ
青空の彼方へ
　　　飛び込む

MELTING THOUGHTS

In wax frames
Lean against the past

Before the sunset
I turn back the clock

ロウソクの炎で
溶けていく想いは
過去にもたれかかり

私は日没の前へ
時計の針を戻す

WHEN SHADOWS FALL

Your presence descends

I gather memories
Scattered to the winds

I LET YOUR IMAGE

Shine to the stars

I'll follow it
At the hour of my death

影が消えると
貴方の姿も退いていく

私は想い出をかき集めて
風の中へまき散らす

私はあなたの面影を
星空に映し出す

私が死ぬとき
私はその影を追おう

PSEUDOCYDONIA*
is changing her dress

I return
Tearing her red skirts
In the burning field

* Flower growing close to the ground

マルメロもどき*
　　が衣替えしている

私は戻って
燃える野原で
彼女の真っ赤なスカートを引き裂く

* 地面すれすれに花をつける

マルメロ　cydonia
熟した果実は明るい黄橙色で洋梨形をしている。花は、大きさは 5cm 程、色は白
またはピンクで 5 枚の花弁がある。Pseudocydonia は偽のマルメロを意味する。

I'M KNEELING
In the corner
Next to a heap of clothes

They have absorbed the past
But remain silent

RIPPING MAGIC APART
You left a knife in the door

How can I stay?

私は跪く
衣類の山の
隅っこで

彼らは過去を飲み込んでいるのに
沈黙のまま

手品を台無しにして
貴方はナイフをドアに刺したまま

このままでいいの？

ON MY KNEES

Bent down to the earth
I touched the shadow
    with my lips

Before scratching into stone
    a sign of disappearance

I wrote down
The history of an empty day

両膝をつき

地面に頭をつけ
私は影に
　　　唇をつける

消去の徴を
　　　石に刻み込むまえに

空しかった日々の歴史を
書き残した

WHEN WE PARTED
Your hands grew white

I walk the narrow streets
      held by you

I STACK
My clothes
A book
A homespun towel

My guilt

私たちが別れた時
貴方の手は白くなった

私は狭い道を歩く
　　　貴方に支えられて

私は積み上げる
私の衣装を
書物を
ホームスパンのタオルを

私の罪を

LAYING THE TABLE

Empty plates
White tablecloth
Sharpness of a knife

テーブルを整える

新しいお皿
真っ白なテーブルクロス
鋭いナイフ

WITH A CLOUD
I wash my face

With the sunset
I dry my hands

ISLANDS ARE SINKING
The colours of earth

The sun comes to a pause
Holding the sea mirror

雲と一緒に
私は顔を洗い

日暮れとともに
私は両手を干す

島は陸地の
彩を沈め

太陽は一息つき
海の鏡をかざす

ONLY SILENCE SPEAKS

Your silence returns in a dream

When we parted you said:
You are all

Deep in my dream
I turn the leaves of books
But avoid their words

語るのは沈黙のみ

貴方の沈黙は夢に戻る

私たちが別れた時貴方は言った：
君がすべてだと

深い夢の中で
私は本の頁をくる
でも頁の言葉は避けている

MY IMAGININGS TOUCH THE SUN

And the horizon does not end
The path of my thoughts

No longer the sea flows but I flow
No longer the sun warms but I warm

And no wave can erase
My imprint in the sand

私の想いは太陽に届く

私の想いの道を区切るのは
地平線ではない

もはや海は溢れず溢れるのは私
もはや太陽は温めず温めるのは私

砂に刻んだ足跡を
波も消すことはできない

I DRAW WHITE SHADOWS
on black ground

The pillow creases into
words of sleep

私は白い影を描く
　　　黒い地面に

枕のしわが
　　　睦言になる

I AM THE SUN
Warming the earth

I am a bird
Flying into distance

I am light
Travelling through space

I am a tree
Branching into the unknown

I am a wave
Never reaching the shore

I am the horizon
Not knowing my limit

I am the world
Belonging to no-one

私は太陽
大地を温める

私は鳥
遠くへ飛ぶ

私は光
宇宙を旅する

私は木
未知の中へ枝を張る

私は波
岸に届くことはない

私は地平線
果てを知らない

私は世界
誰のものでもない

THE WIND
Erased day-dreams

Cut hair
Touched by your lips
   blew on stone

風
が幻想を消し

髪を切り
貴方の唇に触れ
　　石に吹きつける

Author's note:

This selection of poems has been translated and reworked into English by the author from the Lithuanian publications:

The Second Longing (*Antrasis ilgesys*, 1978, USA, AM & M Publications)

Anchors of Memory (*Prisiminimu inkarasi*, 1982, USA, AM & M Publications)

Wind and Roots (*Vejas ir saknys*, 1991, Lithuania, Vaga Publications)

In the process of translation many poems evolved into new poems in English.

著者の注釈

ここに収められた詩は著者自身によってリトアニア語で発表された下記の作品集から英語に翻訳され書き直されたものである。

『二度目の願い』1978、USA, AM&M 出版

『記憶の錨』1982、USA, AM&M 出版

『風と根っこ』1991、リトアニア、ヴァガ出版

翻訳の過程で多くの詩は新しい英語の詩へと進化している。

TABLE OF CONTENTS

目　次

WHITE SHADOWS

白い影

Biographical Note:

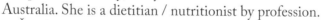

Lidija Šimkutė was born in a small village in Samogitia, Lithuania in 1942.

Her parents fled Lithuania during WWII and arrived in Australia in 1949.

She spent her early childhood in displaced persons camps in Germany, Italy and Australia. She is a dietitian / nutritionist by profession.

Šimkutė extended her studies in Lithuanian language and literature by correspondence through the Lithuanian Language and Literature Institute in Chicago (1973-78) and at Vilnius University (1977, 1987).

She has travelled widely and is published in many journals and anthologies.

Šimkutė has published three books in Lithuanian and one in English / Lithuanian: *Spaces of Silence / Tylos Erdvės*. Other bilingual collections await publication.

She has participated in a number of international poetry festivals and received poetry grants from The Literature Board of Australia Council and South Australian Dept. for the Arts.

Published: three poetry books in Lithuanian, twelve bilingual collections (including translations into German. Polish & six books in Japanese); as well as in literary journals and anthologies in Lithuania, Australia and elsewhere. She also published articles in Lithuania, Australia & USA. Šimkutė's poetry is translated into sixteen languages. She has translated Australian as well as other poetry & prose into Lithuanian and Lithuanian poetry into English. Her poetry was used in modern dance and theatrical performances in Australia, Lithuania, Ukraine & elsewhere. Australian, Lithuanian and British composers have used her poetry for their compositions and performed their works in various venues in Lithuania, Poland, White Russia, Britain and Australia, including Utzon's recital hall at the Opera House in Sydney with the poet reading. She is included in: *Turnrow's Anthology of Contemporary Australian Poetry* (ed. John Kinsella) – 2014;   Prof. J.A.Krikštopaitis - *Lives of Eminent people*, 2016;   Centenary publications: *The Lithuanian Encyclopedia & Who is who*, 2018. www.ace.net.au/lidija

著者紹介

　リジア・シュムクーテは 1942 年にリトアニアのサモギチアにある小さな村に生まれた。

　彼女の両親は第二次大戦中リトアニアを離れて、1949 年にオーストラリアにたどり着いた。

　彼女は幼い頃、ドイツ、イタリア、オーストラリアなどの難民キャンプで過ごした。彼女は今、管理栄養士として働いている。

　シュムクーテは 1973 年から 1978 年までシカゴにあるリトアニア言語文化学院で、さらに 1977 年と 1987 年にはヴィリニュス大学で、リトアニアの言語と文学を通信教育で学んだ。

　彼女は広く世界を回り多くの著作を出版し、多くのアンソロジーなどにも収録されてきた。

　シュムクーテは三冊の詩集をリトアニア語で、『沈黙の空白』と題した一冊をリトアニア語と英語とのバイリンガル版で出版している。同書は薬師川虹一による日本語訳を得て、英語と日本語とのバイリンガル版でも出版されている。なおバイリンガルの詩集が数冊出版予定である。

　彼女はまた多くの国際詩祭のメンバーとして参加し、オーストラリア文化協会や南オーストラリア省などから文学賞を受けている。

Acknowledgments

Some of these poems have been previously published in the following journals:
Aspect, Core, Imagination, Meanjin, Mattoid, Outrider, Rubicon, Southerly (Australia); Emotions, Lituanus, The Poets Guild (USA); Limes (Austria), Vilnius (Lithuania).

Anthologies:
Up From Below, The First Step, Voicing the Difference, Word Tapestry, Friendly Street Poetry Readers 19, 20, 21, 22, 23.

Broadcast on Radio:
ABC Box Seat Programme, 5UV, 5EBI.

Many of these poems have also been translated and published in Macedonian, Italian and Japanese.

I would like to thank David Malouf for his insightful comments; Christian Loidl, Edgar Castle and Peter Eason for their assistance in editing the poems; Slava Karmalita for the artwork and my family and others for their support or assistance in one way or another. A special thank you to Christian for the attentive translation into German.

I want to express my deepest gratitude to Kōichi Yakushigawa.
I'm extremely honoured at his tireless attention and dedication to my poetry. After many years of e-mail exchange, it was heart-warming to finally meet in Lithuania : briefly in Vilnius on his arrival and again later at the Autumn Poetry Festival in Druskininkai – a beautiful resort city. I was amazed and delighted at the instantaneous mutual joy of eye and word exchange of kindred spirits. These memorable short meetings inspired a poem dedicated to Kōichi " YOUR BIRD FLIGHT " / from Kyoto to Vilnius / <…..> which is included with the translation 煌めく風 / Wind Sheen - 2019.

Lidija Šimkutė

Most of The books listed were bilingual: Lithuanian / English /published in Vilnius, except for the last translation into Japanese from " Weisse Schatten / White Rainbows" published in Vienna. In this instance I translated /reworked my poems into English from the first books publications in Lithuanian.

想いと磐 /Thought and Rock - 2014, First published, 2008
何かが語られる /Something is said - 2016, First published 2013
白い虹 / White Rainbows - 2018, First published, 2016
煌めく風 / Wind Sheen - 2019, First published, 2003
沈黙の空白 / Spaces of Silence - 2019, First published, 1999
白い影 / White Shadows - 2020, First published, 2000

謝辞

ここに収録した詩のうちいくつかは下記の雑誌で発表されている。

"Aspect" "Core" "Imagination" "Meanjin" "Mattoid" "Outrider" "Rubicon" "Southerly" (Australia), "Emotions" "Lituanus" "The Poets Guild" (USA), "limcs" (Australia), "Vilnius" (Lithoania)

アンソロジー
"Up From Below", "The First Step", "Voicung the Difference", "Word Tapestry", "Friendly Street Poetry Readers" 19, 20, 21, 22, 23.

ラジオ放送
ABC Box Seat Programme, 5UV, 5EBI。

多くの詩はマケドニア、イタリア、日本で翻訳され、出版されている。

私はデイビッド・マルウフには彼の洞察力に富んだコメント、クリスチャン・ロイデル、エドガア・カッスルとピーター・イースン達の編集作業、スラバ・カルマリータには挿絵、そして私の家族やその他の人々の様々な面での助力など、すべてに対して感謝の意を表したい。クリスチャンには彼の緻密なドイツ語訳に対して特別の感謝を捧げたい。

　リジア・シュムクーテ

Translator's Biographical Note:

Christian Loidl, born in Linz, Upper Austria, in 1957, lives in Vienna. Dr. phil. Published poetry, prose, radio plays, essays and translations. Poet and performer.

ドイツ語への翻訳者略歴

クリスチャン・ロイデル： オーバーエーストライヒ（オーストリア中北部の州）のリンツで 1957 年に生まれる。ウィーン在住。
Ph.D. 詩、散文、放送劇、論文、翻訳など著書多数。
詩人、俳優。

Translator's Postscript

Our world is trembling in fear of the corona-virus. People have disappeared from the streets and confine themselves in their rooms, looking out at a dark sky. Oh, yes. I'm one of them. However, once in a while I sneak out and take a short walk around my house, looking at Mt. Hiei soaring into the sky, looking at the Takano River, where snowy herons stand on one slender leg with their eyes half-closed, like monks. Birds are singing and the soft hills of Matsugasaki are yawning in the sun. All nature is as beautiful as usual, and I love it all. This is my world within myself. This is my identity, my archetype.

'White Shadows' is the sixth book of Lidija Šimkutė's poems I have translated into Japanese, and doing so made me feel alive in the midst of the pandemic. Translation of poetry is never mechanical nor linguistic, but an artistic operation. It is to revive the original in other clothing, keeping the original ambience as skillfully as possible. This means that the translator should be a master of his own language in order to recreate the original world of the poet. Translating Šimkutė's poems into Japanese is always very stimulating, thrilling, and challenging. It always awakens me.

One of the clear elements which makes Šimkutė's poems so exciting is her reticence. Nowadays it seems popular among Japanese poets to coin eye-catching and brilliant words for themselves. As a result, their words seem to be overflowing. Beautiful maybe, but a little vain. When we read Šimkutė's

　このところコロナウイルス騒ぎで、世界中が委縮しているようだ。
おかげで私も出歩かなくなり、家に閉じこもりがちになってしまった。
部屋にこもって小説を読んでいるばかりでは健康に悪いので、時々近
くの川岸を歩く。コロナウイルス騒ぎなどどこ吹く風とばかり、比叡
山はいつもの美しい姿を見せてくれるし、松ヶ崎の丘はのんびりと寝
そべっている。高野川は穏やかに流れ、シラサギが哲学者の雰囲気を
纏ってじっと立っている、一本足で。私はこの景色が好きなのだ。こ
れが私の原風景、原型、なのだという気がする。

　そんな刺激のない生活に堪らなくなって、またリジアさんの詩集の
翻訳に取り組むことにした。これで六冊目の詩集である。私も91歳
になった。去年の10月に『沈黙の空白』を出版してからまだ半年に
ならない。いささかのめり込んでいる感じがするが、それほど彼女の
詩は魅力的だと言える。

　何がそれほど魅力的なのかと言えば、彼女の詩の言葉数の少なさ、
と言えるかもしれない。近頃の詩は言葉数の多い作品が目立つ。私見
で恐縮なのだが、素晴らしい言葉を紡ぎだすことに、いささか詩人自
身が酔っているような感が無きにしも非ず、と思える。そんなときに
彼女の詩は何とも言えない清涼剤になってくれる。

　いや決して単なる清涼剤なんぞではない。メガトン級の爆弾なのだ。
凄まじい破壊力を持った恐るべき無口な詩なのだ。この詩集の序文を
書いておられるクリスチャン・ロイデル博士も多分同感されるだろう。
博士の序文は徹頭徹尾リジアさんの寡黙な世界の恐ろしさ、というか、
魅力について語っておられる。私には付け加えることは何もない、確
かに彼女の詩には、リトアニアの持っている神秘的な世界と、新しく
しかも広大な、オーストラリアという国の持つ広々とした世界とが見
事に融合している、という博士の解説は見事である。だが最後に付け
加えられている博士の日本的沈黙の世界、について少し思うところを
書いてみたい。

poems, we feel as if we have finally found a refreshing drink to cool our thirst. But her poems are not merely refreshing, they are destructive bombs. Her poetry has an explosive power that demolishes clichés.

Dr. Christian Loidl's 'Touching Silence' is a perfect preface to this book. He discusses the essential meaning of her reticence, her silence. No one could add anything to his preface. I agree with him that her poems have Lithuanian mysticism and Australian vastness.

NIGHT AND SEA

Wind and sky
Sun and clouds
    have rejected me

Earth alone pulls
    my hand to herself

Yes, constantly moving nature would never pull her hand. It seems to me that she has nothing to believe in but genius loci. It may be safe to say that the Earth is her other self, or opposing self.

But the Earth has its own skin, and she feels it through its skin. Skin-to-skin contact seems to be the only way for her to feel another self, and yet feeling is something that is lost in words. Therefore, she uses the least, the irreducible minimum. She sings:

夜も海も

風も空も
陽も雲も
　私を拒んできた

大地だけが私の手を
　その身に引き寄せてくれる

と彼女は歌う。そうなんだ、大地だけが、山と川だけが、地霊だけが変わらぬ姿で私の手を取ってくれる。騒がしいだけの人間世界は彼女にとっていかに儚いものかということが肌身に伝わってくるではないか。

　言葉を知った人間は言葉の道をひたすら歩んできた。その道以外に道はないと思い込んできた。言葉のなかった頃、人々に歩む道はなかったのだろうか。

言葉の時代には
肉体は浮いている

幾世紀もの間
言葉と言葉は離れ離れ

　シュムクーテにとって、言葉の時代では言葉は肉体を待たない単なる記号になっている。残るのは饒舌。さもなければ、彼女の場合、可能な限り言葉を切り詰めること以外、書き手と言葉の間に触感という実感を保ち続けることはできないだろう。

私が触れるのは草
木の葉

BODIES FLOAT
In word time

Where centuries
Separate word from word

For Šimkutė, a word becomes a sign without a body in "word
time". There is only garrulity left, or, in her case, using as
few words as possible, because she has kept a natural sense
of touch between the word and the writer.

I touch grass
Leaves of trees
A stone

But yearn
For your touch

She always yearns for real touch without words as a go-
between. Words, which have been worn out, may be
useless. The reliable is the sense of physical feeling. As a
consequence, even names lose their function.

I LET YOUR NAME
Cupped tightly in my hands
Fly into the sky

We have respected Names which identify things around us.
Names have always been with us, and Names have been our
witness. But for Šimkutė, what is indispensable is not Name
but the real and direct sense of touch.

石ころ

　　だけど欲しいのは
　　あなたの肌ざわり

　彼女が求め続けているのは言葉の世界ではない。欲しいのは／あなたの肌ざわり──言葉という徴で媒介される世界ではなく、肌で直に確かめられる世界なのだ。そこには饒舌の入り込む隙間はない。言葉はもはや無用の道具になっている。実感だけが頼りなのだ。身振り、手ぶり、あるいは、ちょっとした目の動き、頬の震え、それが何よりの言葉になる世界。言葉などいらない世界。そこでは名前さえ不要な道具になる。

　　両手の中に
　　捕らえていた貴方の名前を
　　大空に放つ

　今まで私たちは、物に名前を付けることによってそのものを手に入れてきたのではなかったか。名づけることは、その物を理解すること、使いこなせること、ではなかったか。他者としての存在を確認することではなかったか。「名前を大空に放つ」ということは「貴方」という文字としての存在を消すことになる。他者としての貴方は消える。或いは、私と貴方、という区別さえ無用な世界、言葉、あるいは名前という枠組みさえ、彼女にとっては無用な道具に過ぎないのだ。必要なのは「実態」。

　　私は白い影を描く
　　　　黒い地面に

　　枕のしわが
　　　　睦言になる

I DRAW WHITE SHADOWS
on black ground

The pillow creases into
    words of sleep

This is the title poem. Everything is included in it. Words are useless, but the pillow creases. Here is something like Japanese silence, which Dr. Loidl says, "can say so much more than a million words". This is true, but I feel something slightly different. In her poems, there is a real smell, a savor of a human being's real existence. This quality is missing in Japanese silence, which is unreservedly spiritual, or musing, but not physical or sensuous. Lidija Šimkutė expresses a "sense of touch" in vacancy, something that does not exist in Japanese vacancy. This must be the reason why I have been so enthralled by her poems.

March 31st, 2020
Kōichi Yakushigawa

これが表題詩なのだ。すべては此処にあるに違いない。あなたは白い影であり、その実態は枕の「しわ」であり、彼は「しわ」の影なのだ、そして「実存」は影の中にこそ生きている、と言わねばならない。「しわ」がすべてを語っているからもはやそこには煩わしい言葉などいらない。これは昨今話題になっている「新実存主義」とやらにどこか通底するものかもしれない。

　確かにロイデル博士の言う日本的沈黙に似た世界がそこにはある。だがその沈黙は日本的沈黙とかなりかけ離れたものではないだろうか。彼女の沈黙には実存という人間の存在が激しく匂っている。体臭というのではない。「実存」の匂い、としか言いようがない。日本的空白には、それがない。

　肌ざわり、を彼女は空白の中に表現する。日本的空白には肌ざわりがない。徹底的に肌ざわりにこだわる彼女の詩に私が惹かれるのはその異質性のためなのかもしれない。

　Last but not least!　最後になったが決して些細なことではない。中表紙のドイツ語を見て何？と思われたり、後ろのクリスチャン・ロイデル博士の紹介文を読まれておやっと思われた方も多いと思う。もっと先に記しておくべきであったが、リジアさんは今まで彼女の詩集をリトアニア語と英語との二か国語版で編集されてきた。しかしこの詩集の原書は、英語とドイツ語との二か国語版で編集されているのである。そしてドイツ語版はロイデル博士の翻訳によるものであった。念のために付け加えさせていただいた。御寛恕のほどお願いいたします。

令和2年3月31日
コロナに怯える書斎にて
薬師川虹一記

Kōichi Yakushigawa b. 1929 in Kyoto. Poet, translator (incl Phillip Larkin, Seamus Heaney & others, including Lidija Šimkutė's four poetry books,) photographer, professor emeritus. Previous editor of "Ravine" literary journal. On the Board of directors, Kansai Poetry Society. Taught English and literature at Doshisha University. Kyoto. Retired 2004. On the Board of Directors of International Byron Society. President emeritus of the Japanese Byron Society.

Awards: The Kyoto City Art and Culture Association Prize 1997, The Order of the Sacred Treasure, Gold Rays with Neck Ribbon 2010, Translator's Special Prize from Japan Translators Society 2014.

Books published:
Poems; "Cityscape with an old dog" and others
Poems & Photos; Talking with Stone Buddha" and others
Academic; "A Study on the British Romantic Poets and Their Social Background" "Reading the Seamus Heaney's World" and others.

薬師川　虹一

1929 年京都に生まれる。詩人、随筆家、写真家、翻訳者（フィリップ・ラーキン、シェイマス・ヒーニー、テッド・ヒューズ、リジア・シュムクーテ等）、英文学者（イギリス・ロマン派詩人の研究）、同志社大学名誉教授、詩誌「RAVINE」前編集同人。日本詩人クラブ名誉会員。日本バイロン協会名誉会長。国際バイロン協会前理事。

受賞歴：京都市芸術文化協会賞
　　　　日本翻訳家協会特別賞
　　　　瑞宝中綬章

出版書：詩集『疲れた犬のいる風景』他
　　　　詩と写真集『石仏と語る』他
　　　　研究書『イギリスロマン派の研究』他

　　　　翻訳詩集
　　　　リジア・シュムクーテ詩集 / 薬師川虹一訳
　　　　　『想いと磐　THOUGHT AND ROCK』
　　　　　『何かが語られる　SOMETHING IS SAID』
　　　　　『白い虹　White Rainbows』
　　　　　『煌めく風　WIND SHEEN』
　　　　　『沈黙の空白　SPACES of SILENCE』

詩集　白い影

2020 年 6 月 20 日　第 1 刷発行
著　者　リジア・シュムクーテ
翻訳者　薬師川虹一
発行人　左子真由美
発行所　㈱竹林館
〒 530-0044 大阪市北区東天満 2-9-4 千代田ビル東館 7 階 FG
Tel 06-4801-6111　Fax 06-4801-6112
郵便振替 00980-9-44593　URL http://www.chikurinkan.co.jp
印刷・製本　モリモト印刷株式会社
〒 162-0813 東京都新宿区東五軒町 3-19
Ⓒ Lidija Šimkutė
Ⓒ Kōichi Yakushigawa　2020 Printed in Japan
ISBN978-4-86000-434-7 C0098
定価はカバーに表示しています。落丁・乱丁はお取り替えいたします。

White Shadows / poems

Lidija Šimkutė

English-Japanese bilingual edition
Translation: Kōichi Yakushigawa
First published by CHIKURINKAN June. 2020
2-9-4-7FG, Higashitenma, Kita-ku, Osaka, Japan
http://www.chikurinkan.co.jp
Printed by MORIMOTO PRINT CO.,Ltd. Tokyo, Japan
All rights reserved